Diplodocus
The Dippy Idea

Written by Fran Bromage
Illustrated by Richard Watson

WINDMILL BOOKS ™

Published in 2020 by Windmill Books,
an Imprint of Rosen Publishing
29 East 21st Street, New York, NY 10010

© 2020 Miles Kelly Publishing

Cataloging-in-Publication Data

Names: Bromage, Fran. | Watson, Richard.
Title: Diplodocus: the dippy idea / Fran Bromage, illustrated by Richard Watson.
Description: New York : Windmill Books, 2020. | Series: Dinosaur adventures
Identifiers: ISBN 9781725395114 (pbk.) | ISBN 9781725395138 (library bound) | ISBN 9781725395121 (6 pack) | ISBN 9781725395145 (ebook)
Subjects: LCSH: Diplodocus--Juvenile fiction. | Dinosaurs--Juvenile fiction.
Classification: LCC PZ7.B7663 Di 2020 | DDC [E]--dc23

Manufactured in the United States of America

CPSIA Compliance Information: Batch BW20WM: For Further Information contact Rosen Publishing, New York, New York at 1-800-237-9932

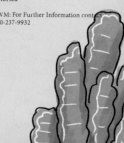

There was once a huge and hungry Diplodocus named Dora.

Dora often had lots of dippy ideas and was easily confused.

2

"Hmm... the best leaves are on that side of the tree," she said one day.

"So I'll stand here and twist my neck like this to reach them!"

3

"Dora! You nearly **stepped on** me!" shouted a small Ornitholestes. "Head over there will you?"

"But my head IS over there," Dora replied, confused.

4

But before Dora could **move away,** an old Diplodocus appeared.

"Sssh! There are Allosauruses about!" he hissed.

5

Dora made herself as **small as possible** and hid behind the nearest tree.

6

She watched as the herd swung their **enormous necks** and tails at the Allosauruses to scare them off.

After the fight, everyone was hungry, but they also wanted to think of new ways to **scare off** the Allosauruses.

The Diplodocus were tired of all the **neck-swinging** and having their meals interrupted.

"We could **disguise ourselves**...as trees," suggested Dora, "with leaves on our heads!"

9

But no one took Dora seriously, so she **wandered off** on her own.

Deeper in the forest, Dora spotted a **Stegosaurus** frightening off another Allosaurus.

10

"You did it!" said Dora, strolling over to the smiling Stegosaurus named Peggy.

"I wish I had super strong plates on my back," Dora sighed.

11

Peggy offered to help Dora make her own plates with mud and palm leaves.

"This is a great idea!" Dora said, smiling. "We'll all look so fierce. No Allosaurus will dare to come near us!"

But **everyone laughed** at Dora's idea and went back to eating leaves.

13

Poor Dora **felt sad** as she wandered down to the rocky shore to wash off her disguise.

"Never mind," said Peggy. "You'll think of something else."

"Er, Peggy?" whispered Dora. "What's that in the **water**?"

Dora plunged her head into the water and looked around.

"Who's in here?" she tried to say underwater (but it came out a little like "blooob-bo-ber?").

16

"I'm Pete. I'm a Plesiosaurus. Are you **coming in** for a swim?"

Dora thought for a moment. She wasn't sure a Diplodocus COULD swim!

17

"Try it and see,"
said Pete.

So Dora found some reeds.
"These will help me breathe!" she
said, and she **dived right in!**

18

"What a good way to
hide," said Dora. "We could
all fit down here!"

"And there's food!" said Dora, trying a big clump of seaweed.

She didn't see the Allosauruses had returned. And she didn't see Peggy trying to warn her.

20

"Peggy! I've got the **best idea**," said Dora. "I think we should... wooooaaah!"

As Dora staggered out of the sea, she fell into a huge **puddle of mud**.

22

She was covered in **thick, drippy black slime**. The reeds, leaves, and seaweed stuck out at all angles.

The Allosauruses had never seen anything so **terrifying** in all their lives!

23

"Well done, Dora!" said another Diplodocus. "Your **dippy idea** wasn't so silly after all!"